For Anders, Corbin, and Tom, my fellow explorers on the expedition of life —K.N.

For my Jonathan, sweet husband and master bug hunter —S.K.

Farrar Straus Giroux Books for Young Readers
An imprint of Macmillan Publishing Group, LLC
175 Fifth Avenue, New York, NY 10010

Text copyright © 2018 by Kate Palaces Narita
Pictures copyright © 2018 by Suzanne Kaufman
All rights reserved
Color separations by Embassy Graphics
Printed in China by Toppan Leefung Printing Ltd., Dongguan City, Guangdong Province
Designed by Roberta Pressel
First edition, 2018
10   9   8   7   6   5   4   3   2   1

mackids.com

Library of Congress Cataloging-in-Publication Data
Names: Narita, Kate, author. | Kaufman, Suzanne, illustrator.
Title: 100 bugs! : a counting book / Kate Narita ; pictures by Suzanne
     Kaufman.
Other titles: One hundred bugs!
Description: First edition. | New York : Farrar Straus Giroux, 2018. |
     Summary: A boy and girl find and count 100 different bugs in their
     backyard in increments of ten.
Identifiers: LCCN 2017010295 | ISBN 9780374306311 (hardcover)
Subjects: | CYAC: Stories in rhyme. | Insects—Fiction. | Counting.
Classification: LCC PZ8.3.N285 Aaf 2018 | DDC [E]—dc23
LC record available at https://lccn.loc.gov/2017010295

SELECTED SOURCES

Eaton, Eric R., and Kenn Kaufman. *Kaufman Field Guide to Insects of North America*. New York: Houghton Mifflin, 2007.

Holm, Heather. *Pollinators of Native Plants: Attract, Observe, and Identify Pollinators and Beneficial Insects with Native Plants*. Minnetonka, Minn.: Pollination Press, 2014.

Nikula, Blair, Jackie Sones, Donald Stokes, and Lillian Stokes. *Stokes Beginner's Guide to Dragonflies*. Boston: Little, Brown, 2002.

Rice, Graham, and Kurt Bluemel, eds. *American Horticultural Society Encyclopedia of Perennials*. New York: DK, 2006.

Our books may be purchased in bulk for promotional, educational, or business use.
Please contact your local bookseller or the Macmillan Corporate and Premium Sales Department
at (800) 221-7945 ext. 5442 or by e-mail at MacmillanSpecialMarkets@macmillan.com.

100 BUGS!

A Counting Book

12/16/2019

Kate Narita

Pictures by
Suzanne Kaufman

FARRAR STRAUS GIROUX
New York

Explorers, explorers,
rising with the sun.

Hat on the creaky door.
Pack on the shiny floor.

It's time for some bug-counting fun!

Walkingsticks, walkingsticks,
hiding all about.

1 by the old hose,
9 by the gold rose.

How many bugs hiding about?

10!

Dragonflies, dragonflies,
zipping all about.

2 by the weather vane,
8 by the bugbane.

How many bugs zipping about?

10!

Leafhoppers, leafhoppers,
hopping all about.

3 by the farrow,
7 by the yarrow.

How many bugs hopping about?

10!

Ladybugs, ladybugs,
zooming all about.
4 by the rafters,
6 by the asters.

How many bugs zooming about?
10!

Bumblebees, bumblebees,
buzzing all about.

5 by the horse feed,
5 by the sneezeweed.

How many bugs buzzing about?

10!

How many bugs out and about?

30 bugs hanging out!

Butterflies, butterflies,
flitting all about.

6 by the rain boot,
4 by the snakeroot.

How many bugs flitting about?
10!

Damselflies, damselflies,
darting all about.

7 by the wishing well,
3 by the coralbells.

How many bugs darting about?
10!

Spittlebugs, spittlebugs,
jumping all about.

8 by the chicken cage,
2 by the woodland sage.

How many bugs jumping about?

10!

Katydids, katydids,
singing all about.

9 by the wood box,
1 by the white phlox.

How many bugs singing about?

10!

EGG CARRIER

NARITA FARMS

PLYMOUTH

Lightning bugs, lightning bugs,
flying all about.

10 by the happy boy,
0 by the autumn joy.

How many bugs flying about?

10!

10 bugs hanging out.

10 from before, plus **10** more. **20** bugs hanging out.

20 from before, plus **10** more. **30** bugs hanging out.

30 from before, plus **10** more. **40** bugs hanging out.

40 from before, plus **10** more. **50** bugs hanging out.

50 from before, plus **10** more. **60** bugs hanging out.

60 from before, plus **10** more. **70** bugs hanging out.

70 from before, plus **10** more. **80** bugs hanging out.

80 from before, plus **10** more. **90** bugs hanging out.

90 from before, plus **10** more. **100** bugs out and about!

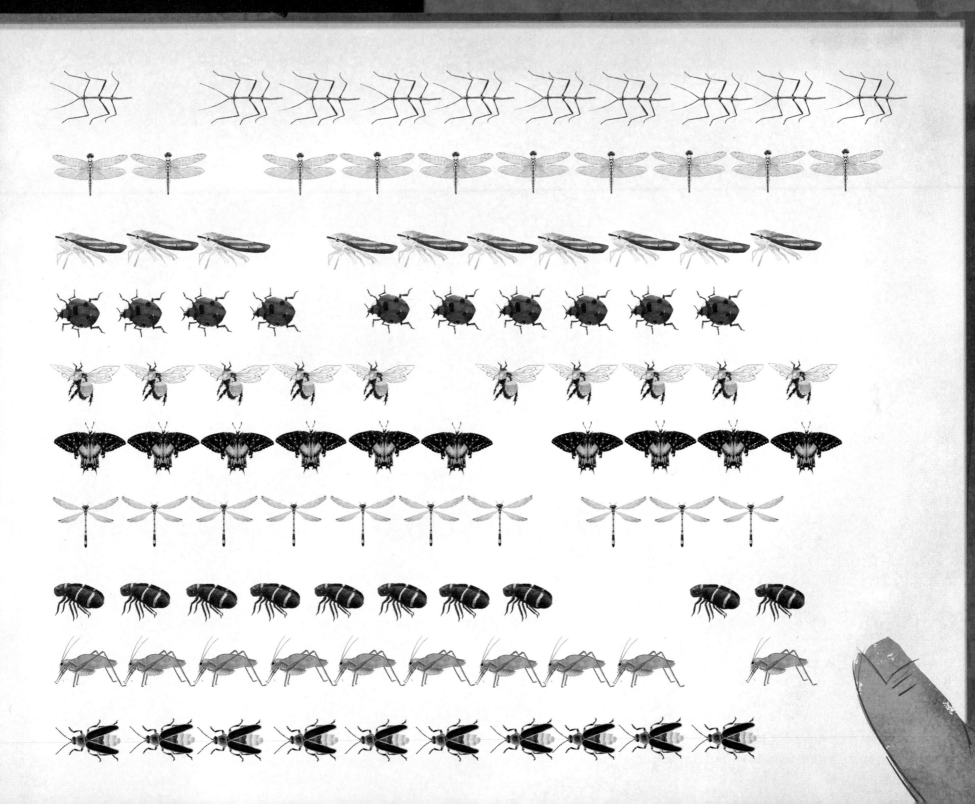

Hip! Hip! Hooray!

It's a 100-bug-count day!

MORE ABOUT THE BUGS

When scientists use the word *bug*, they are referring to Hemiptera, a group of insects that have a sucking, beaklike mouthpart. In common usage, *bug* refers to any insect or other creepy-crawly critter. That's how we are using the word in this book.

CANDY-STRIPED LEAFHOPPER *(Graphocephala coccinea)*

Even though there are more than 20,000 species of leafhoppers worldwide, this true bug marches to the beat of a different drummer. They run sideways, the females are larger than the males, and they shoot their waste far away from themselves to keep predators off their trails.

CONVERGENT LADY BEETLE *(Hippodamia convergens)*

3-2-1 blastoff! In 1999, four lady beetles, also known as ladybugs, flew on NASA's *Columbia* space shuttle so that scientists could see if they could eat aphids in space—just like they do on Earth. They can. Lady beetles were supposed to return to space in 2015 as part of an experiment to see how microgravity affects their life cycle, but the rocket blew up.

EASTERN FORKTAIL *(Ischnura verticalis)*

Damselflies are a lot like dragonflies, but they rest with their wings folded above their backs. Dragonflies can eat prey in mid-flight, but a damselfly dines while perched on a plant.

EASTERN TIGER SWALLOWTAIL *(Papilio glaucus)*

Trick-or-treat! These butterflies wear disguises to avoid predators. A young caterpillar looks like bird poop. The large eyespots on an older caterpillar make enemies think it's a big snake. An adult female's coloring mimics the poisonous pipevine swallowtail butterfly.

GIANT WALKINGSTICK *(Megaphasma denticrus)*

Walkingsticks are wingless wonders that avoid enemies by posing as twigs. If a bird grabs a walkingstick's leg, the leg breaks off from the insect's body. Young walkingsticks can regrow missing legs, but adults can't.

PENNSYLVANIA FIREFLY *(Photuris pennsylvanica)*

Lightning bugs have their own secret code. To attract mates, a male gives off a short green dot of light followed by a longer dash. A female flashes to attract mates, and for another reason—she also uses her light to attract males of other species. Then she eats them!

RATTLER ROUND-WINGED KATYDID *(Amblycorypha rotundifolia)*

Imagine if your ears were on your knees! A katydid's tiny ears are on its legs, but they work just like ours by capturing sound, amplifying it, and transferring the information to the brain.

TRICOLORED BUMBLEBEE *(Bombus ternarius)*

What's all the buzz about? Bumblebees buzz when flying to new places and to shake pollen off of flowers. They also buzz back at the nest. When they fan the air with their wings, it cools off the nest and lets the workers know there's a flower feast nearby.

TWO-LINED SPITTLEBUG *(Prosapia bicincta)*

A spittlebug squirts milky-white goo out of its abdomen and whips it into a bubbly froth. The foamy covering hides the little insect from hungry birds and protects it from the hot sun.

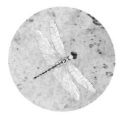

WANDERING GLIDER *(Pantala flavescens)*

These dragonflies really know how to get around. They've been spotted hundreds of miles out to sea and 20,000 feet above sea level in the mountains of the Himalayas.

MORE ABOUT THE PLANTS

AUTUMN JOY (*Sedum telephium*)

Some people trim autumn joy blooms when they wither and dry out. But wildlife lovers don't touch the faded flowers. They know birds will feast on the seeds all winter long.

BUGBANE (*Actaea simplex*)

Bugbane blooms look like tall, white candles, so some people call them fairy candles. Fairies have yet to be seen on the flowers, but scientists agree that butterflies flock to their flames.

COMMON SNEEZEWEED (*Helenium autumnale*)

Don't let the name fool you—this plant won't make you sneeze. So why do deer avoid it? They steer clear of its toxic and bitter leaves.

COMMON YARROW (*Achillea millefolium*)

Talk about an old fossil! Scientists have found 60,000-year-old fossilized yarrow pollen in caves. They disagree about whether Neanderthals or bees transported it there.

CORALBELLS (*Heuchera villosa*)

Producing seeds is not as easy as 1-2-3. In order for a coralbells plant to create a seed, it needs another coralbells nearby. If there are no neighboring plants, there are no seeds.

GARDEN PHLOX *(Phlox paniculata)*

White-tailed deer and eastern cottontail rabbits love to feast on phlox. To stop them, gardeners can sprinkle fox urine around their yard.

JULIA CHILD ROSE *(Rosa 'Julia Child')*

One day after lunch, Julia Child visited Weeks Roses, a rose-growing company in California. She chose this rose to be named after her because the yellow color reminded her of the butter she used in her cooking, and because she liked its licorice scent.

NEW ENGLAND ASTER *(Symphyotrichum novae-angliae)*

An aster is a rest stop for bugs. The flower's petals provide flat landing spots, and its yellow center is like a food court for bees, beetles, and butterflies.

WHITE SNAKEROOT *(Ageratina altissima)*

When cows continually eat small amounts of white snakeroot, they produce milk that can sicken, or even kill, calves and humans. Nancy Lincoln, Abraham Lincoln's mother, died from "milk sickness." Luckily, cows aren't allowed to graze near snakeroot today.

WOODLAND SAGE *(Salvia nemorosa)*

Woodland sage plants attract bees, butterflies, hummingbirds . . . and people, too! That's why this European plant grows in every state, including Hawaii and Alaska.